'Cause She's My Sister

by Nancy Rose Brekke

Rosebud Books
from Raven Productions, Inc

For my sisters,
Bonnie, Lou,
and Julie.
I am so lucky
to have sisters
like you!

For loving sisters
everywhere —
NRB

Printed in Canada
10 9 8 7 6 5 4 3 2 1

Rosebud
Books
from Raven Productions, Inc

More
ROSEBUD BOOKS
by Nancy Rose Brekke

But That's OK
with Grandpa

But Grandma
Didn't Mind

'Cause I'm Momma's
Favorite

I've had a best friend
for as long as I can
remember.
She kind of talks like me,
Kind of acts like me,
and kind of IS like me ...
'CAUSE SHE'S MY
SISTER.

Even though she won't always admit it, I think she was kind of glad when I came along, 'cause then she always had someone to play with. Besides, I was AWFULLY cute.

Once my sister told me that Mom and Dad adopted me. She probably said that so I'd know how much they wanted me. Sometimes she thinks she knows everything, but I don't always tell her that. 'CAUSE SHE'S MY SISTER

And even if I was adopted,
it doesn't really matter,
because my sister and I
are alike in so many ways.
And I fit right
into the family.
'CAUSE SHE'S MY
SISTER

My sister teaches me
a lot of important things
that I really need to know.
'CAUSE SHE'S MY
SISTER

My sister is really
proud of me
when I learn new things.
Sometimes, she
even says so.
'CAUSE SHE'S MY
SISTER

And sometimes when I need a little push, she's there for me. Usually, she's pretty gentle. 'CAUSE SHE'S MY SISTER

My sister likes to
make me feel better.
Once, when I dropped my
ice cream cone,
she let me have
a few licks of hers.
'CAUSE SHE'S MY
SISTER

We like to do lots of other things together.
We even share some of our stuff.
'CAUSE SHE'S MY SISTER

We love to play
with our babies.
Some days I even
let her take care of
my babies.
'CAUSE SHE'S MY
SISTER

When we have
tea parties,
sometimes I let her pour.
'CAUSE SHE'S MY
SISTER

We love to laugh!
We sit next to Mom
and tell her jokes.
My jokes are
the funniest,
but just to be nice,
Mom laughs
at my sister's jokes too.

We go for
walks together.
I like to push the stroller,
but some days
I let HER push.
'CAUSE SHE'S MY
SISTER

We have fun going for rides together, too.
I even let her hold our Siamese cat, Prince.
'CAUSE SHE'S MY SISTER

On special days,
we like to dress up.
Once our brother told us we
looked kinda cute. Maybe
we could even be movie
stars together.
'CAUSE SHE'S MY
SISTER

Mom tells us that we are real characters, so she must think we could be movie stars, too.

We like to wear
each other's
clothes
sometimes.

And she hardly ever complains when I dress just like her. 'CAUSE SHE'S MY SISTER

When we go on vacation,
we have a lot of fun together.
We love to go to the beach.
And I don't ALWAYS
splash her on purpose.
'CAUSE SHE'S MY SISTER

On holidays, my sister and I do most of the decorating. When other family members get in the way, we just wink at each other. She and I know how it's supposed to be done. 'CAUSE SHE'S MY SISTER

When I tell her my
deepest secrets,
she doesn't tell ANYONE,
not even our dog, Buster.

We've had some big adventures. We don't tell anyone else about some of them. But we always tell each other.
'CAUSE SHE'S MY SISTER

Sometimes my sister
gets a little crabby.
Then she REALLY starts
to bug me.

Sometimes we argue.
But we always make up
pretty soon.
If anyone else picks on us,
we stick together.
'CAUSE SHE'S MY
SISTER

Most of the time,
we just enjoy being
together.

I think I'm pretty lucky
to have a sister like her ...
And I should know —
'CAUSE I'M HER SISTER

Here are some of the SPECIAL THINGS
my sister and I like to do together.

_____

_____

_____

_____

_____

_____

_____

_____

_____

Here are some special things
I would like to tell my sister.

Dear _____,

_____

_____

_____

_____

_____

_____

From your loving sis,

_____

Here is a picture of
MY SISTER and me!
(I'm the cute one!)